Hannah Mae
O'Hannigan's
Wild West
Show

to Mom and Dad — parents extraordinaire

with special thanks to Coot

SIMON & SCHUSTER BOOKS FOR YOUNG READERS
An imprint of Simon & Schuster Children's Publishing Division
1230 Avenue of the Americas, New York, New York 10020
Copyright © 2003 by Lisa Campbell Ernst
All rights reserved, including the right of reproduction in whole or
in part in any form.
SIMON & SCHUSTER BOOKS FOR YOUNG READERS is a trademark of
Simon & Schuster.
The text for this book is set in Goudy Old Style.
The illustrations for this book are rendered in pastel ink and pencil.
Manufactured in China   10 9 8 7 6 5 4 3 2 1
Library of Congress Cataloging-in-Publication Data
Ernst, Lisa Campbell. Hannah Mae O'Hannigan's Wild West Show / written and illustrated by Lisa Campbell Ernst.
p. cm. Summary: Born to be a cowgirl, city-dweller Hannah Mae O'Hannigan gets a pony for the backyard
and practices herding hamsters before proving her worth on her Uncle Coot's ranch out West.
ISBN 0-689-85191-X [1. Cowgirls—Fiction. 2. Hamsters—Fiction. 3. West (U.S)—Fiction]
I. Title. PZ7.E7323 Han 2003 [E]—dc21 2002026912

first edition

HANNAH MAE O'HANNIGAN'S WILD WEST SHOW

LISA CAMPBELL ERNST

SIMON & SCHUSTER BOOKS FOR YOUNG READERS

New York London Toronto Sydney Singapore

On the day
Hannah Mae
O'Hannigan
was born,
her dear Uncle Coot
from way out West
sent her a cowgirl hat.

It was then that little
Hannah Mae knew
she would someday be a
rodeo star—the toast of
towns and campfires
around the world.

Much to her parents' surprise, Hannah Mae's first word was "howdy," and she called them "Ma" and "Pa."

Her mother tried dressing her in fancy, frilly clothes,
but Hannah Mae would have none of that. Uncle Coot sent
boots and britches, chaps, and kerchiefs from his ranch.

"Yeeeeha!"
Hannah Mae hollered.
"Cowpoke duds!"

Hannah Mae played cowgirl games, drew cowgirl
pictures, sang cowgirl songs, and read cowgirl books.

As she grew older, her parents grew more worried. "But Hannah Mae," they finally pointed out, "we don't *live* way out West."

And they were right. This cowgirl lived smack-dab in
the middle of a city where cows were as scarce as a snowball
in August. There were no rodeos. There were no cowhands.

"But *Ma, Pa*," Hannah Mae sobbed, "I was *born* to be a buckaroo! I *belong* on the lonesome prairie, tall in my saddle, under the open sky—it's where I'm supposed to be!"

Hannah Mae's parents loved her dearly, and they knew in their hearts she was right.

"Then you'll be the best cowgirl in the world," they said at last. "First you must learn the proper cowgirl skills, then we'll allow you to help out Uncle Coot on his ranch."

And with that, Hannah Mae went into cowgirl training . . . with a few minor city adjustments.

Mr. and Mrs. O'Hannigan wrote Uncle Coot for a list of cowhand skills needed on his ranch:

1. Horse Ridin'

The O'Hannigan's tiny backyard was much too small for a full-sized horse. So, they traded a fancy parlor couch to the pony-ride man in the park, and Hannah Mae became the proud owner of a sweet old pony named Sassafras.

"We're a team now, Sassafras," she whispered in his velvety ear, "come rain or come shine."

2. Ropin'

Hannah Mae read up on roping dos and don'ts in her most recent issue of *Cowpoke Monthly*. She tied together drapery cords, and practiced roping her stuffed animals.

3. Cow Herdin' and General Cattle Care

This was a tough one. Cows, of course, were not permitted in their neighborhood at all, so the O'Hannigans visited their local pet store, and settled on a large group of hamsters.

"How different could they be?" asked Hannah Mae's father.

Despite their petite size, Hannah Mae cared for
them as if they were real cows. She built tiny corrals,
set out feeders and watering troughs, and practiced with
Sassafras herding the hamsters from the kitchen to the
parlor, from the parlor to the library, and back again.

At night she sang cowpoke
songs to settle them to sleep, and
kept tender watch over her herd.

After months of practice, Hannah Mae was a
cowgirl extraordinaire.

One Tuesday morning Mr. and Mrs. O'Hannigan
kissed Hannah Mae and Sassafras good-bye and watched
them board the train bound for way out West.

"Take care of the herd!" called Hannah Mae.

The train carried cargo of all kinds: tools, toys, and treasures—even exotic pets from around the world. Hannah Mae's parents sent a telegram to Uncle Coot: *Hannah Mae on her way to work on ranch. Best cowgirl in the world.*

The trip took four days. Just outside the train station where Uncle Coot waited, a tumbleweed snagged a train wheel.

One of the exotic-pet cars was jolted, spilling its contents. No one knew what had been inside, but Hannah Mae's and Sassafras's ears pricked as they heard the faint sound of tiny footsteps.

When they stepped off the train,
Uncle Coot scooped Hannah Mae and
Sassafras into his big cowboy arms.
"Well, I'll be hornswoggled!" he cried.
"It's the cutest itty-bitty cowgirl I ever
saw with the cutest itty-bitty cow pony
I ever saw!"

Hannah Mae was so happy she thought she'd pop.
"I'm ready for the round-up!" Hannah Mae announced.
"Just show me where to bunk down, and I'll get some
shut-eye before the dawn shift."

"Whoaaa, partner," Uncle Coot said, "I can't let you
out there with them mean nasty cows! *No sireee,* you'd get
squashed like a bug before you could say 'howdy.'"

Hannah Mae started to protest, to tell how hard she'd trained, but Uncle Coot shook his head. "I told your ma and pa I'd look after you, and that's just what I'm gonna to do. I'll give you chores to do on the ranch, but no scalawag cows till you're bigger than knee-high to a grasshopper, and that's that!"

But little did Uncle Coot know what hullabaloo was brewing out on the open range.

In the weeks and months that followed, Hannah Mae made the best of ranch chores—polishing saddles, watering horses, helping the cook in the mess house.

"At least we're way out West," she told Sassafras.

Then one grisly day, never to be
forgotten in cowhand history, Uncle Coot's
roughest, toughest cowboy, Zeke,
came staggering back to the ranch on foot,
his horse spooked, and gone.

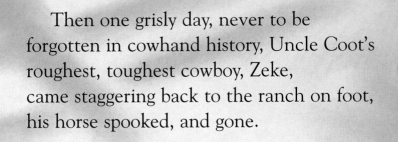

"He's shakin' like the music-end of a rattler," Hannah Mae whispered, fetching a drink of water. The other ranchers gathered round. "*H-h-h-hamsters!*" Zeke sobbed, at last.

And hamsters they were. The spilled train car had been filled with them, and although they started off sweet and gentle, those hamsters turned nasty out in the desert on their own. They multiplied, and got meaner still.

The cowpokes and cow ponies were terrified—never in their wild and woolly lives had they seen such a sight. The cattle stampeded, trying to hide. No one could sleep for nightmares, or eat for fear.

Days passed, then weeks.
Now there were *more* hamsters.

"The ranch is doomed,"
Uncle Coot said sadly, "who
would have thought it'd be
hamsters that did us in?"
And that is when Hannah
Mae came forward. "Excuse me,
Uncle Coot," she said,
"I think I can help."

When Hannah Mae rode
out on Sassafras at dawn the
next morning, Uncle Coot begged her not
to go. "You don't know what you're in for,"
he said, worried. "They're meaner than a
swarm of bees, and twice as tricky."

"Don't fret, Uncle Coot," answered Hannah Mae.
"Just remember: Follow the directions I gave you, and make
sure the ranch hands have things ready when I return."
She kissed her uncle good-bye, and with a whinny from
Sassafras, they galloped away in a cloud of dust.

As Hannah Mae and Sassafras thundered across the open plain, their hearts beat faster.

"Yeeehaaaaaaa!" shouted Hannah Mae into the wind.

But then they saw them: a heap of hateful hamsters on the horizon. The two partners drew closer; they slowed to study the situation. "Those rodents aren't just mean," Hannah Mae whispered, "they're hungry. And thirsty. And scared."

"Come on, boy," Hannah Mae said, and Sassafras swung into action. He whipped around the hamster mob, circling in tight to gather them close. The hamsters began to stampede.

Again, Sassafras and Hannah Mae circled, and then again. But still the hamsters were skittish—a frightening swarm of angry fur balls.

"Okay," Hannah Mae whispered to Sassafras, "we have one last trick."

Slowly, Hannah Mae began to sing.
At first it was barely a whisper, but gradually
Hannah Mae's voice grew stronger:

"Git along, little dogies,
git along, my dear sweets.
I'll take you to water,
and to hamster treats.

"I'll give you sweet carrots,
and red apples too.
Just follow my pony,
we'll take care of you."

The hamsters, one by one, began to settle down, lulled
by the sound of Hannah Mae's voice. After the last circle, the
herd began to follow Sassafras's lead across the open plain.

Back at the ranch, the
cowhands had been busy, building
corrals and troughs to Hannah Mae's
exact specifications. They all gawked
and ran for cover when they saw Hannah
Mae and Sassafras marching across the prairie,
a long trail of wild hamsters behind them. Hannah
Mae's voice was crystal clear every step of the way.

"Open 'er up!"
she shouted at last.

Only Uncle Coot
was brave enough to
step forward and open
the gate of the tiny corral,
but *everyone* cheered as
Sassafras and Hannah Mae
sashayed through with the
hamsters, and the gate
closed with a sturdy click.

That was just the beginning of the cheers. *That* was how it all started. Of course after the hamsters ate and drank and rested, they became as sweet as could be—but no one else would *believe* it. To show how tame they were, Hannah Mae taught the hamsters to do tricks, and before she knew it, cowpokes, ranch hands, even farmers and city people were lining up to see the show.

HANNAH MAE
WILD WEST HA

Trusty Sassafras

Hannah Mae

NOW APPEARING IN HER FIRST WORL
THRILLS, CHILLS AND HERDS OF HERCULE

Then someone started calling it "Hannah Mae O'Hannigan's Wild West Hamster Show," and the rest is rodeo history. Sassafras and Hannah Mae eventually traveled around the world with their amazing herd of hamsters. Mr and Mrs. O'Hannigan came along too. "She's the best cowgirl in the world," they proudly told everyone, and everyone agreed.

But the person who knew that best, of course, was
her dear Uncle Coot from way out West.